YOUR MOTHER WAS A PANTHER

STORIES IN VERSE

Mixon, Tara 1974-

Your Mother Was A Panther / Tara Mixon.

Short Stories.

ISBN-13: 9780692461181

ISBN-10: 0692461183

Printed and bound in the United States of America.

For our mothers and grandmothers—
our children and grandchildren.

& DFM SR.

CONTENTS

MISSISSIPPI VERSUS THE WORLD

Sauda: dark and beautiful; black.

Be cautious when you see
a black woman laughing
it may not be a laugh at all.

When Sauda laughed
it sounded like thunder.

She was a storm threatening
every living thing in her path
a shot gun at the back
of a coward.

She brought her rains and winds
to Medlam Estate and stayed
there for seven days
brought gusts and hail
and the news of emancipation
threatening the crops
threatening the harvest
all of which made
Mr. Medlam mad.

While others ran for shelter
Mississippi remained
at the foot of Sauda dry
not a tear in her eyes.

Mississippi was just a child then
father sold
mother gone
feeding from the lap
of wet nurses when
Sauda came and claimed her.

"I can stop the storms
and save your crops,"
she said to Medlam—
negotiating the terms
of her contract.

"This child
those quarters
fair pay
and the storms
will go away,"
she said.

With no other option
Medlam agreed to her terms.

Sauda stopped raining
and brought an end to the winds
the fawn and flora returned
and the men harvested
the crops in exchange for
shelter and a living wage.

Sauda taught Mississippi
how to garden
how to cook
and catch babies
how to call storms
and send them away
how to sing
her own songs
and pray powerful prayers with
her hands on her hips.

She taught her how
to turn the earth
and grow flowers
marigolds
mums
tulips
and roses without thorns.

Mississippi fed the flowers with
water from the spring
each day traveling
to the water
filling her pail
watching.

The spring
was a gathering place
where white women
adorned in frilly gowns
and fancy hats
lay out blankets and fed
their children from
large picnic baskets.

On the other side
Mississippi worked
filling her pail with water
pulling purple plants
by their roots.

She mastered every lesson Sauda put before her
all but one
she could not hold thunder in her mouth.

From the time
she started walking
till the time of her menses
Mississippi studied at the foot of Sauda
throwing lightning
releasing rain
trying her best to hold on.

Sauda even put her in
a steam tent to
strengthen her
breathing.

Mississippi was meek—
gentle presence
soft touch
a statuesque beauty
with deep set eyes
earthen skin
fingers long enough
to touch the soul
heart pure enough
to heal it.

She tried to hold the
thunder
and failed
tried again and failed
again.

Mississippi would catch it
but it would fall to the ground
barely making a clap.

Once she held it for a full
minute before it escaped
but never longer than that.

Sauda held her storms
until she could hold them no longer.

When she left
she left in the night
headed for high ground
with no promise of return.

She was prepared.
Mississippi had always known
that her mother would leave
but preparation wasn't
enough for the loss of love
abundant.

With Sauda gone
It wasn't long before Medlam
changed his tune
went back to his
old ways
offering the least
asking the most
not knowing.

Mississippi was on her way to the
spring when he grabbed her bucket
and threw it into the bushes.

He dragged her to a thick
area of the woods where
the dirt stung her eyes and
threatened to blind her.

The fallen branches
pierced her skin
her thighs
her back.

She bit down on her tongue
until her mouth was filled with
the taste of her own blood.

He didn't bother to cover his face
so sure of his authority
so certain the storms were over.

Sweat fell from his brow as his
hot breath rushed over her forehead.
Mississippi tried to turn her head to the side
but he pressed his mouth to her lips
and she bit him.
He slapped her.
"You scream and I'll kill you!"

Does she wonder where her husband is?
she thought
as she watched his wife through
a gap in the brush
watched the women
across the spring
as they sat watching
their children at play
fanning themselves
smiling
gossiping
cackling above the mournful sound
of Medlam's belt buckle
she dug her fingers into the ground
and tried to hold on to herself.

When he had finished
he went and retrieved
the water pail.

"Don't you say a damn thing!"

She waited until he had gone back
over to the other side before she
got up and gathered her torn skirt.

She filled her pail with
fresh water
fed her plants
and slipped into her quarters
without saying a word
she went back to catching babies
black and white
black and blue
naked and still.

When she went back to the water
she took lightning with her
keeping the others away
the spring to herself
she knelt down to scoop the water.

Seeing her own reflection
her long thick braids
her smooth black skin
her piercing eyes—
she opened her mouth
gathered the thunder
and held onto it
for the first time.

Awakened from her nest
of protection
she launched a full assault
on her enemies
against Medlam and
the Grasses and the Moss
and the Maple
against the very nature
she hoped would rise up
and protect her—
against the Myrtle Oak that
sat still
and did nothing.

True to her nature
it would come slowly
when Medlam had
almost forgotten
nine months in the
making.

For forty weeks
she danced
as the stars came out
she danced a mournful
uncoordinated dance
that was neither
pretty or graceful.

When it was time
she went into labor
next to the spring.

She sat at the water's edge
eating muscadines and swatting flies
waiting to give birth.

She moved
from one side to the other
and tried all of the same
positions she would suggest
to her laboring mothers.

She thought it nonsense
as her belly quaked
enraged
her waters breaking
flowing over the rocks
and into the spring.

She'd intended to leave
the baby there
for Medlam to come back
and claim his fortune.

Once she delivered the afterbirth
and put it in her pail
she wrapped the baby in
a quilt and placed her beside
the Myrtle.

When she turned to leave
a strong wind rose up and threw her
to the ground.

"Sauda," she called out knowing
and ran to retrieve her child.

The child was brown
her eyes green and piercing.

"Zahra is your name," she said
looking into her daughter's eyes.

Then she opened
her mouth wide
and released
her thunder.

As she passed the main house
on her way back to the quarters
Mrs. Medlam stood looking—
her eyes resting on the green-eyed
child knowing.

"No Missus
It was not your husband.
It was a mulatto boy.
I met him at the spring,"
Mississippi said to the
woman.

"No Ma'am
it was not your husband,"
Mississippi said
laughing.

After she cleaned the baby
and fed her
and dressed her
and made sure she was warm
Mississippi took the
placenta out of the pail
and hung it up.

She turned it daily
for seven full days
until it was
completely dry.

She gathered rocks
from her garden and
scraped the surface
of the dried placenta
grinding it into
powder.

When she had finished
she placed the powder in her pail
and tied Zahra to her back.

She went into the yard
and gave her powder
to the air
she laughed a thunderous laugh
and called up a restless wind
that carried the powder
beyond the quarters
into the fields
out to the spring
and across to the other side.

The spring soon dried
the crops all died
Medlam and the Missus
the Mangoes and Ceders
the Mule and the Myrtle cried out—
begged for a compromise.

Mississippi used her bucket to collect their tears
used them to water her plants before leaving
for the next town
Zahra strapped to her back
Sauda watching from above.

MIDNIGHT

"Grandfather is gone,"
my grandmother said
to my mother.

I watched her
from the bend
of my mother's arm
my head pressed
into the crease.

Something
was different and
my childish uncertainty
had led me to retreat.

My grandmother's face
offered no clues
I did not see the lines
recess into her skin the way
they would when she would
laugh or cry or both.

Grandmother was always slow to speak
but my mother could read her
and I could read my mother.

I looked up to her
for direction
but even she was thrown
not knowing whether
or not my grandmother needed
a nurse or an entertainer.

I studied my grandmother's
face often
her graying eyes
set against perfectly browned skin
looked like raw diamonds.

Her cloud of white hair
pulled into pigtails
a memoir of her youth.

She would tell me stories
a gentle squint of her eyes
revealing whether they were hers
or borrowed.

But that Sunday
they revealed nothing
secret keepers they were.

She sat with her hands clasped
in her lap they looked unnatural
stiff like a tight glove of skin
had been pulled over them
like if she balled them up into a fist

they might split open.

There were no whispers
between the two.
Mother did not question her
as she normally would.

"He black your eye again?"
she would ask.

It was a question absent
the emphasis normally
given to questions.

A question the smallest
observation could answer—
is it black? is it swollen? is it bleeding?

A key in the form of a question
a key that provided entry
into my grandmother's tormentuous world.

She was not required to speak
my mother would handle that.

Some women mourn
when their men leave
whether to death or
to the bed of another woman
but Grandmother did no such thing.

Grandfather had beaten her many times
and many times she'd nursed
the aftermath of his drunken rages
stayed like she deserved that
type of living.

He seemed to hate her
and she seemed to hate him
equally as much.

The cyclical drama made
my own mother angry.

She couldn't bear his reflection
and would stare him down in indignation
when she found herself in his presence.

Her tongue was
a fire only
Grandmother
could extinguish.

"Hush chile,"
she'd say
to which my mother would reply
with a seething sucking of her teeth.

Mother's fiery presence would drive Grandfather
out of the main house and into his smoking shack.

I wondered where she got
the nerve to come up against
such a volatile soul
but she knew better than I
that he would never lay a hand
on his own flesh and blood.

My mother would nurse
my grandmother's wounds
grease her scalp
plait her hair
draw her bath.

Mother was her favorite.

When the other children went North
Mother stayed just a stroll away
from my Grandmother's doorstep.

When I was older
I resolved that I
would never allow
my mother to endure such abuse.

My mother was ironing linens
when I walked into the kitchen.

"Do you have the gift?" I asked her
to which see shot me a look of confusion.

"I know about the gift
the gift that Grandmother speaks of.
Can you call on the ancestors?
Can't you ask them to help Grandmother?
I would not allow you
to suffer like that!"
I blindly said to my mother.

She quickly left my presence
I had hurt her.

Perhaps she didn't have the gift.
Had she tried and failed?

I spent the remainder of
the day at the ironing board
pressing linens.

When I was done
I warmed up some soup
and brought it to her.

She took the bowl
from my hands
and kissed me on my forehead.

I never asked her that question again.

"Where'd Grandfather go?"
I asked naively.

"Go play with Midnight,"
my mother replied.

"Midnight dead,"
Grandmother said
breaking her silence.

"Go outside
child!"
my mother screamed.

I went out
in front of the
slamming screen door
in search of my sweet
Midnight.

When I came back
I found my mother
putting a plate of fried chicken
in the trash.

Midnight!
I cried
and ran with
the type of nervous run
kids do when they try not to cry.

I shook terribly as I
I searched the coop
and the space under
the porch.

I looked behind every watering pan
but I couldn't find her.

I was heartbroken.

Whenever Mother came
to nurse Grandmother
I would abide outside
of their exchange
playing with the animals
holding on to Midnight.

He was Grandmother's
prized black silkie.

Mrs. Waters
the white lady grandmother worked for
had given her Midnight
as a birthday gift
and she had taken special care
to keep him happy and healthy.

He was the strangest looking bird
I'd ever seen.

He seemed to walk upright

and looked more like a fancy dog
but he was a chicken—
not like the white
or brown ones
he was all black
black as night
so I called him Midnight.

And Grandmother said,
"Well, that's his name!"

He was my grandmother's
favorite out of all the animals
and the one she
kept safe from Grandfather.

He would kick
at the other animals
but he knew better
than to lay a finger
on Midnight.

He knew of Grandmother's power
her ability to call up the ancestors
to bring his madness to an end
put him under the ground.

He also knew that she
would never use it for herself.

"It was in my vows," she said.

"I promised I would only use
it once. That's how I kept y'all safe."

She was a woman of her word
but she wouldn't hesitate to
bring the fire if he harmed what was hers.

She spoiled Midnight
fed him special food
and let him in the house.

When he followed her around the garden
she didn't shew him away like she
did the other animals
he was more like a child than a pet.

He'd walk behind her as she hung
her clothes on the line—
right behind her when she took
them down to fold.

And he could tell when
she was ailing
sick or sore
he'd sit down behind
her until she
felt better.

"My mother warned me.
She warned me against him.
came in a dream

ten years dead and told me
not to marry him.
But I didn't listen
and that was the last time
she came to me,"
she said.

Grandmother stopped
talking for
what seemed like forever.

She stared out in the
distance and scratched
her brow.

I sat on the floor
holding onto my jacks
waiting for her to speak
again.

I watched as my mother
shifted her weight onto
her strong leg
never losing her gaze.

"I reckon that's why
she never came back,"
she said—
breaking her silence
pulling at her pigtail.

She laughed
and a tear fell down
her cheek.

I'd never seen
my grandmother cry.

I ran to her in what must have been reflex.
"You all right, Grandmother?" I said
pulling her hands to my face
kissing them.

They smelled like bleach always
Grandmother cleaning
doing laundry
wringing out the clothes
with her hands—
the right hand twisting forward
the left twisting back
two hands
same body
in opposition.

"Grandma *be* fine—
just got a lot of things to mourn.
I took a lot but I never let him hurt y'all.
I would've killed him myself,"
she said.

"Not a hand on y'all children
not a hand on Midnight.

Those were my conditions
that's all I asked."

My grandfather was never mean to me.
He never talked ugly
to me or my mother like
he did to Grandmother.

He spoke to me gently
like I was the adult
and him
a child—
like I could absolve him.

He had a way about him
that almost made me forget
what a tyrant he was.

I would go with him
when he went to play the numbers game.
They called it Bolletta.

Grandfather would give the
Bolletta man his numbers
and a couple dollars.

He always liked to take me
with him when he went
to play the numbers because
I was his good luck charm.

"When is your birthday?"
he would ask
like he'd forgotten
10-16-74
and he would play those numbers.

Whenever he had a few extra dollars
he'd study the signs
looking for numbers as
we walked into town.

I liked walking with Grandfather.
He took short steps
so I didn't have to run to keep up with
him like I did when I walked with
my mother or grandmother.

"Thirteen, thirty…"
and play those numbers too!

He couldn't read words
but he knew his numbers
and could count his change.

When we'd get to that little blue house
he'd have me wait outside.

He didn't want me to see
what was going on
but I knew
everyone knew what went on

in the little blue house.

I'd just sit there kicking rocks
until he came back out—
smiling.

He always seemed so hopeful
like a man with a big dream.

He'd come out with
his hands intertwined
engaged in his own little prayer.

That game couldn't have paid
much more than a hundred
dollars.

When he would hit
he would peel off
one of those dollars
and give it to me.

Then we would walk
to the liquor store
and he would get himself a drink
and me a chocolate milk soda
and we'd walk home together
just as happy.

I had never seen
him angry.

I had only ever witnessed
the aftermath
until that last time.

He was certain his number had hit
there was a look in the
Bolletta man's eyes that Grandfather
couldn't shake
add to that the fact that Grandfather wasn't able to verify
that anyone in town had won the pot.

When he went back in to question him
the Bolletta man smirked
and that angered Grandfather.

I could hear him cursing from my spot out front.
I stopped kicking rocks
and thought about running
but Grandfather came out and picked up
one of the big rocks.

He threw it right at the man's head
breaking the skin between his eyes
a stream of blood trickled down his face
and he fell to the ground.

Grandfather grabbed my hand and didn't look back.

We didn't stop at the liquor store
we just walked home.

He held onto my hand
and whistled like he did
whenever he was nervous.
In his other hand
he held the money
he'd taken from the
bleeding man.

"It was Ol' Red and his son,"
my grandmother said.

I sat quietly at the door
listening.

"They didn't wear
no hoods—
neither one of them.

But them others—
maybe five of em—
they was covered.

Couldn't see nothing more
than their eyes.

They pushed in the
front door and
took it right off the hinges.

Grandfather screamed
and ran off into the woods
with his pants in his hand."

"They caught him on the pot,"
my grandmother said
wiping the sweat from her lip.

I thought my mother would've
jumped for joy
but she kept her eyes on my
grandmother
hanging onto every word.

She seemed to mirror her.

If Grandmother cried
Mother's eyes would well up.

If she laughed
my mother would giggle.

Reflect
my mother would go
back too.

My mother didn't
ask any questions
she just stood there
waiting for confirmation.

"He won't be back,"
Grandmother said
cupping her hands
over her knee caps.
"I knew if I cried out
to the ancestors
if I used my magic
just once
he would be gone
forever."

"He knew how much
I loved Midnight
but he was so hateful—
plain old evil!"
she said
slapping her thighs.

"There's nothing left of him
'cept for his clothes
and shoes burning
out behind the coop."

"Come home with us,"
my mother said
to my grandmother.

"Nope. I'm gonna stay right here
in my home.
I'll be fine,"
my grandmother replied.

"I'm gonna take me a
hot bath
read my bible
and go to bed."

"Maybe Mama
will come tonight
and visit me in my dreams,"
she said.

My mother helped
my grandmother undress
and get into her soaking tub.

I went to Grandfather's
smoking shack
to say my goodbyes.

I was glad for my grandmother
and only a little sad for myself.

She had finally used her power
called on the ancestors
and Grandfather was
gone
gone

gone.

I never told them
how I found midnight
quietly sitting in the corner of
Grandfather's smoking shack.

Or that I had taken him out
into the woods
and left him there.

Grandfather was gone
my grandmother was at peace
and that's all that mattered.

LYING EYES

July 4 1985

Today is my sister
Nissi's eighteenth birthday.
I'm eleven.
My birthday's in September.
I'm almost twelve.
When I'm twelve
nobody can tell me nothing.

When I told Mama that
she said
"You'll have more privileges
but, no
you won't be grown!"

That doesn't make
a whole lot of sense to me.

Twelve is darn near grown.
Besides
I'm wearing training bras now.
And when I got my period last summer
mama said
"You're a woman now."

That pretty much settles it for me
but then mama said,
"Within reason..."

What the hell does that mean?

Anyway
I don't usually cuss like this—

I mean
I say ass sometimes
but Nana says ass
ain't no curse word.

It's in the bible.
I saw it myself.

Nissi keeps telling me
"Only in context..."

That don't make no sense either.
If it ain't a curse, it ain't a curse!

How can folks be grown
and without sense at the same time?
I ain't gonna be like that.

So Nissi's eighteen
Whop-te-do!
Mama says that means she's a grown
woman now.

She can come and go
as she pleases.

She can eat what she wants
without somebody
telling her it's too much.

She can kiss boys
and smoke funny
cigarettes too!

Mama didn't say that
but Nissi does it
and she tells me
all kinds of stuff
grownup stuff
because I'm so mature.

Nissi's so lucky!

I can't wait until I can do as I please.
Mama watches me like a hawk.
I tell her I'm almost twelve
but that ain't enough for her.

She says she doesn't want me
running the streets
like those other kids.

I ask her why?
And she says
"Because I said so."
or
"Don't question me!"

Most times she just
looks at me real intent
with her lips tight together
and don't say nothing at all.

I know not to keep asking
but under my breath
I talk about how I can't
wait until I'm grown
till I can go as I please
and kiss all the boys I want.

Nissi's got herself a boyfriend

I saw them making eyes at each other at the field
when she was supposed to be watching
me and Baker and Ty
but she didn't pay us no mind.

She didn't even see Ty slip that a dollar out of her wallet
and she won't ever know if she wait on me to tell her.

That's what she get
walking 'round all grown and proud.

Her and that boy was behind the dugout staring into
each other's eyes—kissing and rubbing.

I stood there watching them until Ty knocked me up
side my head with the ball.

When I get to be grown,
I'm going to marry Jimmy Daniels
and kiss him whenever I want.

July 5 1985

Today me and mama went to pick up
grandpa Joe from the AmVets.

Like always
he was as drunk as Cooter Brown.

He brought a woman with him.
She was drunk too!

She stumbled something awful—
walked like one leg was longer than the other.

It looked like that left leg would get stuck
every third step or so.

Joe held on to her so hard that there was
no chance of her falling.

When they got to the car
Joe had the biggest smile on his face.
He made mama reach over
and roll down the window
so he could introduce her before
they got in.

"This is my woman,

Her name Esperanza," he said
attempting to roll his
R's like the Spanish folks do.

With only two front teeth
all mama got was a shower of Joe's stinky spit.

"She coming home with me,"

he said to mama.
"She's pretty, ain't she?" he asked.
But mama didn't say a word.
I didn't either—
cuz she wasn't that pretty.

She had a face full of moles like folks have freckles.
They weren't flat like freckles though.
They were raised like bumps
and all different sizes—
reminded me of stars.

She sat down in the back seat beside me
and I sat quietly studying her face
trying to find the Big Dipper.

Tomorrow's the last day of school.

When I come back from summer vacation
I'll be in the seventh grade.

Junior high is almost like high school.

The only difference is that
in high school they can drive cars
and smoke cigarettes on their lunch break.

Mama did my hair.

It took almost the entire day.

First she washed it
then she detangled it
and braided it into sections
then she went back
and unbraided each one
blow dried it
and then braided it back.

"That keeps the hair from
knotting on itself," she said.

After she finished all the sections
she took a chair into the kitchen
and sat it there next to the stove
while she heated the hot comb.

I snuk away to get a snack.

I finished the sandwich
but I only got one bite of my apple before
she called me to sit back down.

All I could do was sit there
and watch my apple turn brown
because mama doesn't allow no eating
while she's pressing hair.

She says
"One wrong move and your forehead's burnt."

That's what happened to Tameka Jones.
She had to walk around with
a Band-Aid on her forehead
for a whole week.

I didn't want that to happen to me
so I sat as still as I could.

Ain't nothing pretty about a burnt forehead.

The pressing comb got so hot
I could smell the heat.

When mama went a little
heavy on the grease
I could hear my hair frying.

The kitchen filled up with so much smoke
that I could hardly keep my eyes on my apple.

After mama finished pressing
she wrapped my hair up
in sponge rollers and a bonnet.

I told mama
"Beauty sure does take a long time."

And she said to me
"Child,
this ain't your beauty.
this is only your crown."

Yeah.
She said that.
I don't have a clue what
she's talking about.

I ain't no queen and
boys don't care one bit
about a crown.

July 8 1985

Now that school's out,
I spend the days with Joe
and his girlfriend
Esperanza.

I think she's a little too old
to be a girlfriend
but mama says every woman's got
a little girl inside her.

That doesn't make much sense to me.

When I get to be grown
I'm going to be all grown.

Anyway
when I see Esperanza
I try to roll my R's like Joe
but they get stuck
and I just sit there rolling
for a minute or so
before I can sound out the last part.

Esperanza sits there

watching me
laughing.

I ask her if I can call her
something else.

She says
"No. Call me by my name!"

Then she tells me
"Don't worry about the R's.
Joe's the only one that does that."

July 9 1985

Nissi didn't come home
last night
and mama's mad.

I ask her why
since Nissi's grown?

She tells me to stop mouthing off
and doesn't answer me.

I know where she is
but I don't tell.

Grown people should be able to have secrets.
That's what I think.

Besides
I might have told her
if she didn't look at me so mean
when I asked my question.

While we drive to Joe's

I sit there wondering about
what Nissi's doing.

Lots of boys and men like Nissi
They say she fine
got a nice shape
pretty
and stuff
like that.

Even the old men try
to rap to her
when she walks by.

They sit on the porch
all day smoking and drinking
and playing cards.

I don't know what
makes them think Nissi
would have anything to do
with they old asses.

Half of em ain't even got
a full set of teeth.
That's just nasty!

I walk on the other side of the street
till I pass them.

Mama says

there's lots of stuff more important
than being pretty.

Sometimes I want to ask her what
else but I think she might just look
at me with her tight lips or something.

Today
her face was a little softer
so I took the chance.

I asked her
"Mama what's wrong with a boy
telling a girl she's beautiful?"

Mama took her time answering me.
She didn't normally do that.

But this time she sat there
at the red light
thinking.

Then she turned and looked at me
right in the eye.

She said,
"Nari Rose
You are the smartest little girl I know
—pretty too

But your mind
is what makes you
beautiful."

Then she said
"Be cautious of
people who call you
beautiful before you've
ever spoken a word."

And that was that.
Mama really meant what she was saying
because she looked me in the eye.

Mama only looks people in their eye
when she's serious.

Like when she had to tell Joe that his sister
Nookie had passed
or when Mudear found the lump
and the doctor's had to operate.

I still want to be pretty when I get grown
but I'll also try to remember what mama said.

July 10 1985

Esperanza took to sitting in a chair.
She says the sofa's too soft.

That don't sound like nothing I ever heard.
But then again
I ain't never seen a woman shaped like Esperanza.

Her backside is so square
It's a wonder Joe don't cut himself
when he grabs her like he does.

Always got his hands on her—
like she his doll or stuffed animal.

Esperanza's more like one of those
Lego people though.

That's probably not a nice thing to say
but I can't think of no other way to describe her.

She's a funny
looking woman.

Her face is long and skinny.

Her mouth looks like somebody drew it on
like Olive Oil on the Popeye cartoon.

She towers over Joe

but that ain't saying much
everybody towers over Joe.

Mama said Nissi was looking
at the top of his head before her twelfth birthday.

I haven't been so lucky
I mean
here I am
almost a teenager.

I keep asking God to make me taller
but He's taking his sweet old time.

Baker and Ty say there's a secret
etched on the top of Joe's head
and Baker and Ty hardly ever lie
that much.

Nissi's so difficult about it
She say
"I can neither confirm or deny."
How ridiculous!

Anyway

I have never seen a black
woman look like Esperanza
I told her that too.

Well
I didn't tell her like that
Mama would tan my hide
if I did.

Instead I said
"You're not like Joe's other women."

Then I realized after I said it
that what I said was just as bad.

I could tell by the look on her face.

She drew her mouth up
just like mama does when she's mad.

Then she put both her hands
on those square hips.

Looking down at me
she said
"That's because I ain't no regular black woman.

I was born in Nairobi!"

She stomped her feet

when she said it too—
like it was supposed to mean
something to me.

"I don't know where that is," I said.

I wasn't trying to be fast
or disrespectful or nothing
I really didn't know.

But that made her mad
I could tell by the way she
sucked her teeth
loud and slow.

It made me scared
because I didn't want her to tell Joe
so I got right in front of her
so I could look her in the eyes
like mama does when she's serious.

I asked her
"Esperanza, where is Nairobi?"
When I asked her
I could see her face soften
her sunken jowls plumped up
she lifted her head all proud.

"Nairobi is in Afrika!" she said.

July 13 1985

Nissi came back home yesterday
but she doesn't seem the same.

She barely talks.

When mama asks her questions
she gives her one-word answers.

Mama hates one-word answers
but she doesn't push.

I got up early this morning
I can't wait to get to Joe's
to see Esperanza.

She tells me stories about Afrika
about how she lived in the village
with her mama while
her daddy was in the Army.

Mama doesn't believe her
but I do.

I tell mama that I want to go to Afrika someday.

"To which country?" Mama asks."

"Afrika," I respond—
mad that she made me say it twice.

"Afrika is not a country, Nari Rose.
Afrika's a continent,"
she says to me.

"I know mama,"
I say to her.
But I really don't know.

I want her to keep on thinking that I'm smart
and beautiful on the inside.

Esperanza taught me
how to play Tunk today.
She shuffled the cards real fancy
I watched her separate them
into two stacks
and when she put the two together
they moved the air like a fan.

When she left the room
I tried to make them fan
but the cards just flew
all over the place.

We played Tunk until it was time for lunch.

She wears a tube top

and I see a scar on her chest
like Auntie's polio scar
but raised like
a volcano
like if it were mad enough
it would
erupt ugly.

I wonder if she got it in Nairobi
but I don't ask.

When I hug her
I lay my head on her
chest on purpose

I rub my cheek
against her scar
it feels soft and
hard at the same time.

She smells like Joe's Old Spice.

I don't think she's ugly at all

I'm ashamed of
myself
my eyes
betrayed me.

I wonder how many other
beautiful things
I missed when I had those lying eyes.

Joe cooks

these little hard
dry burgers
with onions in em.

I hate onions
I always have to pick them out
before I eat.

He makes
homemade french fries too
they could choke the great beast.

I like Esperanza's lunches better.

She makes my grilled cheese sandwiches
with lots of butter.
Then she sits and watches me eat.

I tell her how much I love her
sandwiches but she just goes
on about how good Joe cooks—
talking real loud so he can hear.

We both know she's lying.

July 14 1985

I got to Joe's early this morning
but Esperanza wasn't there.

I asked Joe where she was
but he wouldn't answer me.

I could see in his eyes that he was drunk.

His eyes look a little lazy when it's quiet
but when somebody says something
they perk up and look like they just seen a ghost.

I keep my distance when Joe's drunk.

Nissi came to get me
early on account of Joe's condition.

All the adults act different today.

They don't say much
so I just keep to myself
and pray that Esperanza comes back soon.

I miss her grilled cheeses and her stories.

July 15 1985

Mama says I have to stay home today
I ask her why
but she doesn't answer.

Nissi stays home too
she tells me that Esperanza's hurt
and that Joe did it
then she swears me to secrecy.

I tell her I'm tired
but I'm not
I just want to get in the bed
and cry.

I feel sad for Esperanza
I ask God to keep her safe.

July 16 1985

Esperanza called
for mama to pick her up
from the hospital.

Her leg is broken
and she walks on crutches.

The nurse helps her into
the seat next to me.

I try to stay still
and not look at her too hard
but she shakes my leg
and smiles at me
I can't help but to smile.

I think to myself how beautiful she is.

Mama asks Esperanza
where she wants to go.

Esperanza tells her that
she's going back to Joe's.

That makes me scared for her
I don't understand
Mama doesn't either.

"Are you sure?"

mama says.

Esperanza tries to speak
but no words come out.

She nods her head and I watch
as her little lips tighten up
and start to shake.

She can see the
worry on my face.

"I'll go home soon,"
she says to me.

"To Afrika?" I ask
But she doesn't answer me.

Joe's at the door when we get there.

He's smiling and happy
jumping around like its Christmas.

He thinks we don't know what happened.
But I know and I don't say nothing to him.

On the way back home

I ask mama why
Joe's not in jail.

She says they only gave him
a slap on the wrist.

I don't understand.
Mama says it's an idiom
"It means they didn't give him the
punishment he deserves."

Idiom's are stupid.

July 30 1985

I haven't been to see Esperanza since
she came back from the hospital.

Mama says
it's better if I stay home for a while.

I want to ask how she's doing
but I'm afraid of the answer.

July 31 1985

Mama bought me
an encyclopedia today.

She got it with
her Green Stamps.

It tells you everything
you want to know about
things that start with the letter A.

I couldn't wait to look up Afrika.

The encyclopedia says that
Afrika is the world's second
largest continent.

It has over fifty countries and
hundreds of languages.

I tell mama what I learn.

I watch her eyes dance as she tells me
how smart I am
It feels good
I wanna tell her more
so I can see her eyes dance again.

I can't wait to tell Esperanza what I learned.

August 1 1985

Mama took me to see
Esperanza today.

Said she was tired of
seeing me mope around sad.

I told Esperanza what I learned about Afrika
she asked me if I learned about Nairobi
I told her it will be a while
before mama has enough
Green Stamps to get to "N."

We played Tunk
and watched Wheel of Fortune.

Esperanza looked different today
The whites of her eyes were real yellow
not white-white like mama's and mine.

August 10 1985

Esperanza's been vomiting
all night.

Joe called mama
this morning
asked if she could come
take her to the doctor
but Esperanza won't go.

She keeps
talking
about home.

I ask her if
she misses Nairobi.

She tells me
Nairobi's just a story
says she was born in Georgia.

I'm not mad at Esperanza
I just want her to get better
I tell her that.

She says
"I have to go"
I don't know what she means
but the look on mama's face tells me
it's not good.

August 11 1985

I know Esperanza's from Georgia
but I can't stop reading about Afrika.

I started keeping track of mama's
Green Stamp booklet.

One more stamp and we'll be able
to get the next encyclopedia.

August 15 1985

Nissi and that boy broke up.

She caught him
cheating with ol' ugly Cynt
from Richmond Heights.

She cries a lot.

Mama asks her if she seen her period lately.

She says, she hasn't.

Mama says
"That explains it."

I know what that means—
like when they said Creda swallowed
a watermelon seed before she had little Tom
but I don't say nothing.

I just sit and think about Esperanza.

I've been practicing my Solitaire
and I want to show her how good I am.

August 16 1985

Mama brought home the "B"
encyclopedia just in time.

I had already finished the first book
and was starting to panic.

I'm still practicing my Solitaire.

August 18 1985

Botswana is a country in Afrika.
It's mostly desert.
The people there speak a language called Setswana.
I wonder if Esperanza's ever heard of Botswana.

September 1 1985

Esperanza's been sleeping for two days
When we try to wake her up
she just throws up her hands
and moans
we can't make out what she saying.

"She's feverish,"
mama says.

Joe sits beside her with a cold cloth
wiping her head.

He looks like he's scared.

I think he loves her
then I think about it some more
and I decide that it can't be so.

He would never have broken
her leg if he did.

Maybe he's scared she'll die
and come back and haunt him.

Joe says he's gonna call
the ambulance
if she doesn't wake up soon.

I watch her from the hall
I never saw anybody so sick
I ask God to take her pain away
I ask him if he'll let her see
Nairobi before he takes her to heaven.

September 2 1985

Esperanza went in her sleep
that's the way Mama put it
she thought it be easier to say that
rather than say she died
but that's what happened
she died.

I never knew anyone that died before
I just sit there with the grownups
sad as me.

I hold it together the best I can lest they
see me crying and cry even harder.

Esperanza's children don't come right away
they come the next day
I didn't even know she had children
she never talked about em.

Her daughter looks just like her
but lighter
her son is real tall and lady-like
he wears a purse and talks with his hands.

Their faces look blank
like they don't feel nothing.

I can't stop my heart from beating loud
It feels like it's in my throat.
I feel sad.

I miss Esperanza already.
I miss playing cards.

I miss her stories about Afrika
even if they were just stories.

Her children

ask Joe for her watch
and for her necklaces
and fancy things
did she have insurance?
yes
she had insurance.
how much?
they don't ask for her clothes
her shoes
or her Bible
all I want is her deck of cards
I take them
and shove them in my pocket when nobody's looking.

September 7 1985

Cameroon is in Central Afrika.
It gained its independence from France in 1960.
The president's name is Paul Biya.

I miss Esperanza.
I wonder if she can see me?

September 15 1985

Today's my birthday.

Mama asked me what I wanted
for a gift.

I told her that I'm almost done
with "C."

Mama smiled when I said that.

She made my birthday cake from scratch
she even put twelve candles on top
twelve is a lot of candles to have on a cake
they made such a big fire
when I went to blow them out
I could feel the heat under my chin.

Nissi told me to make a wish.

I asked God to let me stay
a child
for a long
long
time.

OLA SHUN AND THE REBIRTH OF ILL

Ola Shun walked with a boombox
on her head—
in the same way some
Zulu women carry food
or clothes
or water
to their families.

It rested atop a bun she'd
formed with her braids.

She walked
with a gentle rhythm
a cadence that called
for an accompaniment
of soul or jazz or blues
but the radio was off.

She got it from her mama—
the walking
the walking with
her work on her head—
from her mother
Sadiq
who walked the door down
as a missionary
before she met
and fell in love
with Ola's father
Sam
before Sam fell in love with Sadiq's
sweet sugar
rhythmic soul
booty serving in the back
life-giving in the front
turning tables
on their ones
and twos
and don't stop
till you get enough
and all that
"Stairway to Heaven"
O'Jays
Here We Go."

When Ola was born
they fed her
Motown and
Baraka
"Les Fleurs"
and Variations of
Huey
Davis
Rapp.

She cut her teeth
on her daddy's 45s
and her mama's 33s
Sam's chicken and okra
Sadiq's fried cornbread
her parent's sweet love
the bump
Sam touching Sadiq's hips
in wide open spaces
Sadiq grinning
wide when he
came home
Marvin Gaye
Sugar Hill Gang
De La Soul
De La Soul.

Summers in the sprinklers
listening to Earth
Wind and Fire's
"September."

Makeshift Slip 'n Slides
with dollar store pool floats
walking on water
sliding on water.

Ice cream trucks tagged
with goodies
Push Ups
Chocolate Éclairs
Now and Laters
sweet
Lemonheads
sour
pork skins
pickled eggs
and Red Hots.

Asking mama for
a dollar
okay
fifty cents
daddy coming to
the rescue
buying her
anything she
wants.

The large wooden spoon
and fork on the kitchen wall
crocheted butterfly magnets
on the refrigerator
Nana's greens cooking on the stove too long
Aunty's green Tupperware full of potato salad
Uncle on the grill burning the hot dogs
her daddy dancing to
Parliament
her mama laughing
mouth wide open.

Sam was more Monk
more Mingus *Ah Um*
sometimes Davis *Kind of Blue*
he could rock with
Jungle Brothers and
Tribe but he loved
Parliament
Mothership Connection
Motor Booty Affair
Chocolate City.

Sadiq more
Chaka Khan
more Con Funk Shun
Soul Train
Solid Gold
dancing with Ola Shun late
on school nights.

Photos of Sadiq
and Sam at the club.

Sadiq sitting in a
high back rattan
chair—
Sam posing on one knee
fist resting on his chin.

Late night love sessions
pillow over her ear
slightly
listening
to her parents
black love.

Sadiq singing
Stephanie Mills on
Saturday mornings
cooking pancakes
in cast iron
pouring
Alaga syrup
on top
slab bacon
eggs with cheese
cheese grits
and toast.

Sadiq singing
Donna Summer
"Let's dance"
painting her toes
Sam on the floor
holding her foot
blowing the polish dry.

Sadiq braiding her hair
with thin remnants of
Ankara—

Her and her mama's
Willona and Penny
kinda love.

Dancing on the table
breaking on the floor
mama and daughter B-girls.

Sadiq ill
fighting
strong face.

Mama be all right.
We gon' beat this.

Traditional medicine
Experimental therapies.
"What's Going On?"
"Is This The End?"
Five boys singing—
What do they know?
This is grown folks business.
"Nightshift"
Commodores.

And unto Ola Shun I hereby bequeath:
Last Poets
Black Thought
Common Sense.

She left the Earth fighting
kissing Sam long and
hard first.
"Endless Love"
on repeat.

'till the record warped
and he played nothing at
all—

And Ola
Radio silence
I hear you talking
but you ain't sayin nuthin:
Uncle Luke
Repeat
Misogyny
Repeat
Broken Records
Repeat
Black Booties
and Breast
Repeat.

A teenage love—
Donnie from Hillside.

NBA Jersey
Nets snap back
high top Js
smelling like Cool Water.

Back rubs
sweet love
"Bonita Applebum"
dope instrumentals.

Bodies touching in wide
open spaces
her grinning wide
a little bit
a whole lot
a little bit more
her two weeks late
him grinning wide
a lil bit.

Ola Shun
walking with the boombox on her head
ripped acid-washed blue jeans
and a cropped top
iron pressed iron-on letters.

Front: Rap Killed Hip Hop
Back: !

Her mama's dashiki as a jacket—
split down the middle
waist beads around
her waist
showing off her baby bump.

Hands on her hips
eyes locked on the horizon.

Ignoring the greetings
of her neighbors.

Mrs. Jennings who she'd
normally wave to in the
mornings.

Ignoring Jack as he
approached her for change.

Miss Edna who she'd always
allowed to kiss her cheeks.

The children whose
snickers met her at every corner.

She walked down the ave
past the Good Samaritan Church
past the Masjid and the high school
past the guys on corners
exchanging obscenities.

She was almost to the highway
before she stopped
reached up and
flipped the FM dial
bumped the volume up
and went back to walking
adjusting her feet to the
beat of the music.

Walked all the way
to the bordering town
past the drunks sitting in front
of the liquor store
past the pizzeria
and the Caribbean-American Grocery.

When she reached the road
just before the highway
she ignored the red hand
on the crossing signal
and walked right into the street.

A white Cadillac jumped
the curve to avoid hitting her.

The driver shouted obscenities.

The men watched from the liquor store
some with their mouths hanging open
and others with their eyes covered.

A young girl outside
the laundry mat screamed
so loud she scared her
own self to tears.

Ola Shun walked to the middle of the overpass
and adjusted the volume once more
closed her eyes and felt the music.

With her back to the highway
she stood
arms akimbo
tipped her head backward
and allowed the boombox to
fall down into the traffic below—

"Come back correct or don't come
back at all!"

WHEN GREY WAS BLACK

Blue Black

When I was black
my mother would sit on the sofa
and I would sit on the floor
on a cushion between her knees.

She would braid my hair
blue magic bergamot
greasing my scalp
pulling my strands
parting them
into neat rows.

She would pick out her
own afro so big
it made
white folks like
my father
uncomfortable.

Mother as mirror
Mother as measure
Mother as affirmation
My mother,
Hadari
was black

and beautiful
and regal and timeless.

When my mother left
I didn't know who
to be.

With a white father
who saw no color
who saw division
in the braided hair
adornments and the other
cultural accoutrements
my mother left behind
the things I was trying
to hold onto.

He gave me
shelter and stability
academia
love.

But my mother gave me
art and jazz and poetry—
Sister Sonia
and the wonderful sounds
of Brother Stevland.

I read them
I played them
Long—after she was gone.

Off-Black

When I first met Keisha
I knew that we would be friends
she was the only other
other in our school.

She couldn't braid hair
but she had a cousin
who had a cousin who
braided hair over on the East side.

We took three buses to get there.

And I took a page I had torn out of one of my
mother's old copies of Ebony Magazine
November
1979.

A photo of Cicely Tyson
with her hair braided into
a regal crown.

"This is what I want,"
I said to Keisha's cousin's cousin.

Seventy-Five Dollars and
two hours later
my hair looked as good as
the photo but my head hurt
more than I'd remembered.

My head throbbed and
the skin on my face was tight
pulled up like I'd had a facelift—
my eyes so slanted
I looked more Asian
than black.

When I got home
after midnight
my father barely
recognized me.

I never expected my father to
like the braids
he didn't
neither did
administration.

I was forced
to take them out
before I could go
back to school.

I wanted to go back
to when me and my mother
were black
and Nigerian
strangers in America
others in our own home.
I cried in
my mother's memory

from the pain of
taking them out
three strands
in reverse—
my head no longer
throbbing.

I had lost
like I'd lost my
lonely petition for
Afrikan-American history classes at school
to speak my mother's tongue
in our home.

I was tired of losing.

I'd followed my mother's murals
to a building just a block
North of Third Avenue
but there was no sign of her.

I began to doubt the
prophecy I'd been given over
a cappuccino and chocolate scone.

"Keisha can't be trusted," I said
as my feet sank into a small
mound of dirt and ice.

I hadn't called my father
I didn't know what to say.

I had taken the money from
his wallet
enough to miss
not enough to break him.

I wondered what he was thinking
but quickly dismantled
the unwelcome
chatter of my conscience.

He had to know this
would happen.

What did he expect?

I traveled
two days by bus
to get to the city
and walked what
seemed like hours
searching
for some sign
of my mother
clutching a single page
an illustration she'd left
behind—
an early draft of the murals
that had made the national news
the same murals that colored
many of the old buildings
in the city.

I followed a
vacancy sign to the end
of a lonely alley where I feigned
warmth beneath the pink
glow of the building's neon sign.

It revealed a familiar image.
Carved into the brick—
Hadari's mark
a weather worn etching that matched
the illustration on the page I held in my hands.

With my free
hand I banged on the old
steel door
it opened outward clipping
the top of my shoe

A man stood silhouetted
looking every bit the lead
part of a nightmare.

"Hadari?"
I asked—too tired to say more.
"Who?" he answered.
"The artist," I said—
pointing to the etching
holding up the drawing.

"The woman who made
this! I'm looking for her."

"She ain't lived here in years,"
he said
stepping into the light.

My legs threatened
to give in.

He lit a cigarette
inhaled and blew the
smoke into my face.

"Her daughter still lives here,"
he said.

"Daughter?"

He took another puff
before answering—
blowing that one
into my face too.

"Yeah. She works at night
though. Be back in the morning,"
he said.

Weather worn with
my condition quickly declining
I could not give in to the
shock of this new information.

My own preservation was the priority
at least for that moment.

I needed food
but my lonely pack
of animal crackers would have to do.

I needed warmth.

"Do you have any vacancies?"
I asked—
catching him just as he began to close
the massive door.

"I have twenty for the night," I said.

"Twenty dollars will only get you concrete,"
he replied—
eyes dull and motionless.

His bottom lids drooped
to reveal their inner lining
the whites and the reds.

I shifted my attention from the man
to my mother's marking
while he spouted off a list
of non-amenities.

"Concrete?" I asked—
hoping by some miracle concrete

was the name of the building
the street, or even the owner
—Concrete Jackson?

"Concrete floor," he replied.

An unfurnished
uncarpeted room
was all twenty dollars
would afford me for the night
a night that was nearly over.

"It'll be forty tomorrow
if you want to stay the day," he said
his eyes never departing
from their lifeless gaze.

He held them
with an intent
that suggested he had attached
his life savings to one
never-ending game of stare.

I watched as his lower lip flopped over
tirelessly seeking separation from his face.

His bottom lip was whetted with what
looked like a tear.

It was a single drop of spittle
that hung there suspended.

Below it
my father's twenty-dollar bill
dangled helplessly.

The stress of the intense
negotiations made my palms sweat
just like Hadari's would when she
was nervous or angry.

At times
it was hard to remember her
but I held on to
a small collection of black
and white scenes.

I played them on repeat:
Thanksgiving in Martha's Vineyard
Christmas at home
Easter
Hadari leaving—
and her hands
moist
whenever bills were due
checks slow
whenever Father was at home
my mother's palms would sweat
and she would nervously dry
them on the legs of her
dungarees.

I was always searching for traces
of my mother in my own being
and they would show up at the
darndest times.

It was always my mother and me.

I had resolved that
she'd left because she had
no other choice
that her very existence was an offence
that she'd been exiled for.

But the thought of Hadari having
another family
weakened that resolve.

I had never imagined a sister.
I instantly wanted to hate her
like I hated my father's family:

the ones who offered obligatory hugs
the ones who outright hated my blackness

the ones who used me as their trophy

even the ones who loved me
in spite of my resistance.

I had always only wanted the one person
who continued to allude me

Hadari
silhouetted
at the end of a narrow hallway.

Hadari in floral pedal pushers
a Benjamin Banneker tee
and a worn leather jacket
her thick mane fighting to constrict
my view of the sun.

Hadari riding off on
her motor scooter—
afro free to the wind.

"Your father is much too limiting, Greylon."
she said to me
her weeping child.

"You'll know
this for yourself soon enough,"
she said tapping the tip of my nose.

As a child
I would sleep with her photograph beneath my pillow.

I would study
her face
her strong nose
eyebrows
tracing my own face for similarities.
By now she would
be in her fifties
likely still looking the part of a teenage mother.

There was no telling
how long it would take to find her
a twenty-dollar room
was all I could wager.

I had strategically distributed
my father's money
in case I was
mugged or picpocketed:

two
hundred dollar bills
shoved into my sock
another two
pinned in my bra
and the last hundred
I put in my pockets:
eighty in the left and the other
twenty in the right.

It was over this twenty
I negotiated.

The super's hand
grasped one end
and mine
the other.

"It's all I have," I pleaded.

"In the cities
they do it that way"
my father had said—
reciting small nuggets of prose
contrived street etiquette
he'd gleaned from
movies and books.

Now that I'd breached the
perimeter and left him to his
daily habit of wheat toast
Earl Grey tea
lecture halls
and undergrads
his words were like
haunting whispers.

*"Don't let them know how
much you have."*

"I'm sure
you have at least one room with a bed,"
I said to the super—
attempting a scowl
but in the cold
my lips felt contorted
and they shook uncontrollably.

Unable to intimidate the man
I gave in
just as his spittle claimed the twenty for itself.

I released the dampened bill
and watched as he
folded it into his pocket.

Parting with twenty
dollars had never been as difficult
as it was in that moment.

The other bills
in their varying safe places
felt much lighter than they had before.

The man led me
down a steep set of stairs
to the basement of the old building.

The paint had worn off the walls
and only a few patches remained.

I dreaded seeing the
condition of my
twenty-dollar room.

Scratches on the old
banister revealed that
it had at one time
been blue
then green
and yellow
before its most recent
coat of brown.

As I descended
the stairs
my feet sunk
into the warped boards.

Halfway down
I lost my
balance and began
to fall.

I clutched the rail with my hand
picking up a sticky
substance as I regained my footing.

"You'll learn where the sweet spots are,"
he said,
as he waited for
me to reach the bottom of the stairs.

He laughed with his shoulders
bouncing them up
and down for effect.

His eye's remained fixed
but he managed to tuck in his bottom
lip before a second drop of spittle made
it's descent.

The door to my twenty-dollar room was heavy
it was covered in green faux leather
with gold-tone nail heads around its perimeter
and the emblem of a snake and cross
the space had once been an
examining room in a doctor's office.

In the center of the floor
I could see indentations from
where an examining table once sat
I wished it were still there
It would've made a fine bed.

"I guess I've hit the big time,"
I joked as I surveyed the room.

"There's a shower on the third floor,"
the super said as he closed the door.

The building was deep
in the throes of the city
tucked into a side street
with a mix up of dollar stores
auto repair shops and
launderettes—
nothing like home.

"Trust no one,"
my father's voice again.

His words penetrated
as I lay curled beneath a
small pass through that
had once been used
to transport urine samples
and other specimens.

"Dammit, Hadari!"
"A daughter? Is that why you left?

Were you ever real?
Had I simply imagined you?"

Hadari as a figment of my imagination
Hadari as an apparition
Hadari as a fallen deity?

I was chasing
a faded image on loop.

Hadari in her floral
pedal pushers riding off in the sunset.

I had left home
in search of my mother's garden
only to land in a city
made of concrete.

Before daybreak
I was awakened by
knocking
I crawled over and pulled
myself up by the handle.

I opened the door
to find a young woman who
looked like Hadari.

Blacker

I'm Nnenna
I'm your sister," she said
embracing me.

"I've been expecting you,"
she said at a volume no one would
appreciate at such an early hour.

Sister? Thief?
The one who stole Hadari?

I slipped out of her grip
and covered my face with my hands
removing the sleep from my
eyes before I responded.

"I feel like I should invite you in
but as you can see
I have no place for you
to sit," I said to her.

"Nonsense!"
Nnenna replied.

She laughed, exposing a flirty gap.

I moved with caution
grabbing my backpack and scarf
twisting at the sleeves of my trench
searching the room for a distraction.

"Awww. Come on, sis," she said
grabbing my hand
practically dragging me up to the third floor.

Her windows were dressed in
bright yellows and oranges
a strong contrast against the dark
clouds beyond them.

I rested my eyes on a couple of
handmade dolls
as she danced into
the adjacent room.

Nnenna was livelier than I had
expected with what little expectation I
could produce in the few hours
since I'd been made aware
of her existence.

I wondered what
knowledge Nnenna had—
why had she expected me?

As I sat awkwardly on the sofa
I took a visual accounting of the room's contents

looking for some sign of my mother.

Amongst the carved figurines
Maasai beads
Kente cloth and
Nigerian flag
I found a photograph
of me and Hadari
and a girl
slightly taller than me
was that her? Nnenna?

Taken on our last day together?

My mother was wearing the same outfit
the pedal pushers
the jacket.

Had I forgotten?
edited and deleted her
appearances?

"I'll make breakfast as soon as I shower,"
she said.

I was hungry
my stomach rumbled
but I didn't want to eat.

I was still tired
I tried to catch a moment of sleep

tried to find a comfortable position
on the sofa amongst the many Dutch wax
print pillows and throws.

"Now, time for breaky," Nnenna said
crossing into the small kitchenette
freshly showered
her body wrapped in cloth.

Her scent was familiar
similar to my mother's.

Through a crack in the door
I'd watch my mother dress
prepping her skin with rosewater before
massaging it with almond oil
and vetiver.

Nnenna had the same
earthen skin as Hadari.

"I know you have questions.
I'll tell you as much as I know
but first, breakfast,"
Nnenna said
flashing me a quick smile.

She pulled her hair into
a bun and wrapped it in cloth
before she began
slicing up plantains.

I tried again
to sleep
laying my head on a stack of pillows
I barely exhaled before my
rest was interrupted by the
sound of Nnenna cooking.

She danced as she sliced fruit
danced as she cooked
she even danced as she placed the
dish of collards in the microwave.

It was five in the morning
and she
moved with the grace of
a bullfrog—
a terrible cacophony of
pots and pans.

I could not
for the life of me
fathom what business
anyone could have that required such
commotion.

Perhaps she'll allow me rest
after we eat, I thought.

I made my way to the small
bistro table where she had
prepared a breakfast of fried

plantain, fruit, collard greens
and cornbread.

"I'm older,"
she said to me
as she pressed her cornbread
into her collard greens
eating it with her fingers.

"You were just a little girl
the last time I saw you,"
she said.

"I didn't even know that we were
sisters. She didn't tell me until
after we were gone."

Collard juice ran down her hand
and she sucked at her wrist
catching the stream
lest any drop go to waste
like some priceless potion.

"Ummm,"
she exclaimed,
as if someone other than her had
prepared the food.

I'd had collard greens and cornbread at
Keisha's house
many times but

I had never seen anyone eat them
with their fingers.

I sampled the collards with my fork.
The taste was familiar but not pleasant.

I thought of eating them with my hands.
Would that make them taste better?
But I didn't want to mock her.

I ate the plantain and the fruit and
listened to her talk.

"She left my dad for yours.
She left me too
and didn't come back.

I don't know if she ever would have come back
if my dad hadn't passed away.

She stayed a good while before
she left again."

"I'm sorry. I--didn't know," I said.

"How could you?
You didn't even know about me,
right?"

"Not before last night,"
I said through a shifty grin.

"Well. It is what it is.
You know what I mean?
Thank God there's only
two of us," she said
with a chuckle
laughing
then crying
before laughing again.

Fade to Black
"I was a child. She just rode off on her bike
like I didn't matter."

"We rode off," my new sister said—
editing herself back into my life.

"Sometimes we have to leave something
behind to become who we are,"
she said to me
her little sister
who still hadn't
called her father.

TWO-THOUSAND ONE

She lay there completely naked
her entire soul on display.

She could still feel his
imprint
the warmth of his lips
on her thighs.

"You cannot go,"
Alyce whispered.
"Ranthac comes at eight.

He'll be here blowing
his horn shortly.
What will I tell him?"

Before
she could ask again
she was startled by the movements of the
child she carried within.

They had named him
Mumbai.

Miles liked the vibration
of the name on his lips

Mummmm Baiiii.

He wanted to die
at home on God's terms.
And she agreed
to honor his wishes.

She would forego the chest compressions
the impulse to place her lips over his
to breathe her own life into his body
he did not want that
but he agreed to her remedies
the flax oil and fresh pineapple in his porridge
flax oil, fresh pineapple, and cottage cheese on his salad.

The sound of
Ranthac's horn
shook her and
Miles out of *her* sleep.

She gathered a length of Ankara
and tied it around her body.

"Not today," she said through a crack in the window.
"Not today," she said again, shouting.

"The world's on fire!"
Ranthac returned.

"We're under attack!" he yelled—
leaving as frantically as he'd arrived.

"That was him," Alyce said
to her resting husband.

"He's gone now,"
she said turning on
the television.

"Your son is busy
this morning.

He's been angrily kicking
my bladder.

I've gone to
pee five times already."

"It's almost time,"
Miles said,
eyes still shut.

"Mumbai will come today,"
he said in exhale.

"Don't worry.
I've already met him.
He will come and I
will go."

His hands
were still warm
his breathing slow
and labored.

He did not pull the air
into his body as freely as
he normally would.

But there was a peace about him
that distracted her from
her own selfish thoughts.

She wanted him there
had not accepted the inevitable.

She was fiercely independent—
a student of Sister Walker's
School of Womanist Studies and
Professor of her own ruminations.

There was nothing she needed from him—
he was a want that could be there or gone without
any injury to her ego
to her self worth.

Miles had been a choice
like state college
grad school and her brief stint in seminary.

She had made a choice to love him
and marry him
and carry his child
in the face of death.

She had done it all
because she wanted to.

But as she watched him
she thought about how
desperately she wanted
him to stay and how
much her intense wanting
felt like needing
like her own breath leaving
her body.

She would miss the way
he passed his
fingers over each of her
nails as she slept—
watching her dream
kissing her
to wake
lying in the cuff
of his arms pretending
to be asleep
breathing in his exhale
kissing the strong bridge
of his nose
playing with the hairs of
his knotty goatee
him shaving off her tired locs
kissing her bald head
making love to her fully exposed
and playing like
juveniles:
hide and seek
tweedle le le
hopscotch
spin the bottle
just because
It was always
him.

She had never loved
anyone to the degree
she loved Miles.

She was strong in her
resolve unwavering
in her ability to gauge her
lack and find remedy
to embrace her own contradictions
what was hers was hers.

She would never get to
fall in love with him
as a father.

Dreams of them both sitting
Afrikan style
silhouetted—
him holding Mumbai
smiling
her looking at him lovingly
were only dreams.

She could hear it
the news in the background
the panic in the voices.

She would soon live
half alive

raising a black boy
alone

in a new Amerikkka

the smoke
the impending attacks

the whites of his eyes
now xanthic

the
end
near.

Alyce tried
to muffle her sobs
to subdue her body's instinct to quake
she wrapped herself into him
taking his head in her arms
she could feel the heat of his breath
upon her breast
couldn't help but to
issue one final plea
one more dose of flax oil.

Miles could sense her
determination
could feel the trembling of her soul.

"Do not move,"
he uttered, flailing his eyes open
and shut in one succinct motion.

"I won't,"
she whispered quietly.
"What can I do for you?"
she asked
as a dark cloud of smoke rose
up behind their home.

He struggled to move his head
like he had more to say
but couldn't.

I'll stay here with you,"
she said
passing her fingers over his forehead.

She did not want him
to leave her she
hated the uncertainty
of when and where and how
their bodies would come undone
hearts lose their syncopation.

She had chosen to make
revolutions around him
for a lifetime tried to
hold her breath
to wrap herself into him
keep the family together.

"My grandmother built
this house
I told you before
didn't I?
She built it with
her own hands.
She danced the tiles
into position.
You think I'm being funny
don't you?
It's true.
I saw it myself.
In a dream

I saw it.
The first waters that flowed
through the faucets
came from her own tears.
It's fanciful, isn't it?
Say?
You'll meet her soon."

The plane hit
the second tower
the broadcaster
reported with
measured speech

the country was under
attack
her world was falling
apart

skin to skin
draped in her fabric
she struggled to warm his cold
body
to resuscitate her love

she
pressed her lips to his
and exhaled into him
for the last time.

Ten

You were late
for the show
and they were upset.

You knew they would be.

But they didn't know
You had fallen that night.

Nine

minutes before five.
You showered
and dressed early.
You would meet the
postman in the lobby.
You had Your ID ready.
You signed for the tickets
and rushed to grab a taxi.
They wouldn't imagine
You'd be on Your
way long before
they made
the bus transfer
on 61st.
Even as he pressed
his way beyond
the layers You'd saved
for that unknown
suitor, You thought of
Your two sisters standing
on the corner of
4th and Foster
in wait for You.

Eight

Heels would have looked better
with Your Ankara shirt dress
but You wanted to be on time
so You put on the Adidas
and threw Your Via Spiga's in Your bag.
You were an hour ahead of schedule
when You took a left on Spencer.
You wanted to give them the
opposite
of what
they expected:
Harlem Late
Harlem explaining
Harlem apologizing—
"Why are black people always late?"
Your sister You would
tease.

Seven

But before that
You would stop
at the bodega on
Willow—
for flowers
the single stemmed roses asleep
in the fridge
tucked into their own
plastic vases
—Your mind was filled with visions
of Your two sisters standing
before You
their mouths agape.

You would flash a clever smile.

The old Filipino man
ahead of You
was slow counting his change.
It cost You a few minutes
so You took a chance
on the alley behind 11th.

Six

"Where's Harlem?
Shit
Where's Harlem?
She always does this.
She swore to me she
would be here,"
Aminat yelled.

She was angry
of course she was
she paid for the
tickets.
She was there early
Fatima
would be there soon.
They would expect You to be late
but You had other plans.

Five

Was he someone You'd seen before?
In passing?
At the mall
the rally for
Black Lives?
Had he stood beside You
fist in the air?
Was he there when You
passed out
free meals in the park?
Behind You
at the concert
screaming
Yes
Yes
Y'all?

How many women
had told him no that night?
Maybe not just no

but

Hell No!

Laughed
or smirked
questioned his
audacity
made fun of his
receding hairline?

He would show them.

But why You?
When there were women walking
just two blocks down.

Cheap bastard.

Four

You cried out to Black Jesus
As he pressed his elbow into
Your collar bone
kicked Your legs open
bruised Your hip
pressed Your throat
in
holding onto the two
single buds
squeezing the tubes
till the water spilled out of the top
onto his face.

If he killed You
would they ever find Your body?
—

A dimly lit staccato
screaming out to silence.

Three

You pulled the
Via Spiga from Your bag
and pounded the heel into his
eye socket.

You were angered by his yells.
Who was he crying out to?
Did he expect a savior?
You were the only one there.

"Bitch!"

You screamed as You
rolled his sweaty
body off of You
grabbed Your bag
and ran leaving
a single shoe
behind.

Two

You listened to Coltrane
on vinyl
as You washed the scrapes
on Your knuckles
burnt by the soapy water
by the smell of him
dripping
from inside You
Your sisters wept
for an opportunity
that would come
the next time
the sun passed over
Your building.

It was eight o'clock
when You finished
showering
for the second time.

Your sisters paged
You frantically.

One

It was
One a.m.
when You finished
showering
for the
seventh time.
One o'clock
when You finally
answered
the phone
One o'clock
when You apologized
and offered
reparations
One o'clock
when Your sister yelled
obscenities
and slammed
the phone down
on the receiver.

le début.

www.ingramcontent.com/pod-product-compliance
Lightning Source LLC
Chambersburg PA
CBHW020657260626
47157CB00008B/3072